THE
MAGIC
GOLD FISH

Henry Holt and Company, Inc.
Publishers since 1866
115 West 18th Street
New York, New York 10011

Henry Holt is a registered
trademark of Henry Holt and Company, Inc.

Published in Canada by Fitzhenry & Whiteside Ltd.,
195 Allstate Parkway, Markham, Ontario L3R 4T8.

Library of Congress Cataloging-in-Publication Data
Demi. The magic gold fish / by Aleksandr Pushkin; adapted and illustrated by Demi.
Summary: A poor fisherman's greedy wife is never satisfied with the wishes
granted her by an enchanted fish. This version is adapted from Louis Zelikoff's
translation of Pushkin's "The tale of the fisherman and the little fish."
[1. Fairy tales.   2. Folklore.]   I. Pushkin, Aleksandr Sergeevich, 1799–1837.
Skazka o rybake i rybke. English.   II. Title.
PZ8.D3994Mag   1995   [398.2'09470457—dc20   94-48934

ISBN 0-8050-3243-6
First Edition—1995
Printed in the United States of America on acid-free paper. ∞

1   3   5   7   9   10   8   6   4   2

The artist used traditional Chinese inks (with powdered jade for good luck) and
Cel-vinyl paint to create the illustrations for this book.

The
MAGIC
GOLD FISH

A RUSSIAN FOLKTALE BY

ALEKSANDR PUSHKIN

ADAPTED AND ILLUSTRATED BY

DEMI

HENRY HOLT AND COMPANY

NEW YORK

There once lived an old man and old wife
By the shore of the deep blue ocean.
They lived in a tumbledown hovel
For thirty-three summers and winters.
The old man caught fish for his living,
And his wife spun yarn on her distaff.

He once cast his net in the ocean,
But caught only mud from the bottom.
He twice cast his net in the ocean,
But caught only pieces of seaweed.
He thrice cast his net in the ocean,
And caught one small fish—but a Gold Fish!
The Gold Fish began to implore him,
And it spoke with a real human voice:
"Put me back in the ocean, old man,
I'll give you whatever you ask me!
I'll pay you a great royal ransom!"
The old man was scared and astonished—
He'd been fishing for thirty-three summers
But not once had he heard a fish talking.
With care he untangled the Gold Fish
And tenderly said as he did so:
"God bless you my dear little Gold Fish!
Go back to your home in the ocean
And roam where you will without hindrance."

To his wife the old fisherman hastened
To tell her about this great marvel.
"I caught only one fish this morning,
'Twas an uncommon treasure of gold.
It spoke like a person and begged me
To put it back into the ocean,
And promised to pay a rich ransom,
And give me whatever I asked for.
But how could I ask for a ransom?
I freed it without any payment."
His wife started scolding the old man:
"Oh, you simpleton! Silly! Great fool!
Couldn't ask a mere fish for a ransom?
Not even a measly washtub?
For ours is all falling to pieces!"

The old man returned to the seashore,
Where blue waves were frolicking lightly.
He called to the magical Gold Fish.
The Gold Fish swam right up and asked him:
"What is it, old man, you are wanting?"
Then bowing, the old man did answer:
"Forgive me, Your Majesty Gold Fish.
My old wife has scolded me roundly.
She says that she wants a new washtub
For ours is all falling to pieces."
The Gold Fish then smiled, as he answered:
"Very well then, you'll have a new washtub,
Don't worry. Go home. God be with you!"

To his wife the old fisherman hastened,
And there was a sparkling new washtub!
But she scolded him louder than ever:
"Oh, you simpleton! Silly! Great fool!
To ask for a measly washtub!
Return to the Gold Fish, you silly,
Bow down, and then ask for a cottage!"

Again he went back to the seashore,
And this time the blue sea was troubled.
He called to the magical Gold Fish.
The Gold Fish swam right up and asked him:
"What is it, old man, you are wanting?"
Then bowing, the old man did answer:
"Forgive me, Your Majesty Gold Fish!
My woman is madder than ever—
Won't leave me alone for a minute!
She says that she wants a new cottage!"
The Gold Fish then smiled, as he answered:
"So be it—she'll have a new cottage.
Don't worry. Go home. God be with you!"

The old man returned to the seashore.
The ocean was restlessly foaming.
He called to the magical Gold Fish.
The Gold Fish swam right up and asked him:
"What is it, old man, you are wanting?"
Then bowing, the old man did answer:
"Forgive me, Your Majesty Gold Fish!
My woman is madder than ever—
She gives me no rest for a second!
She's tired of being a peasant,
And wants to be made a Fine Lady."
The Gold Fish then smiled, as he answered:
"Don't worry. Go home. God be with you!"

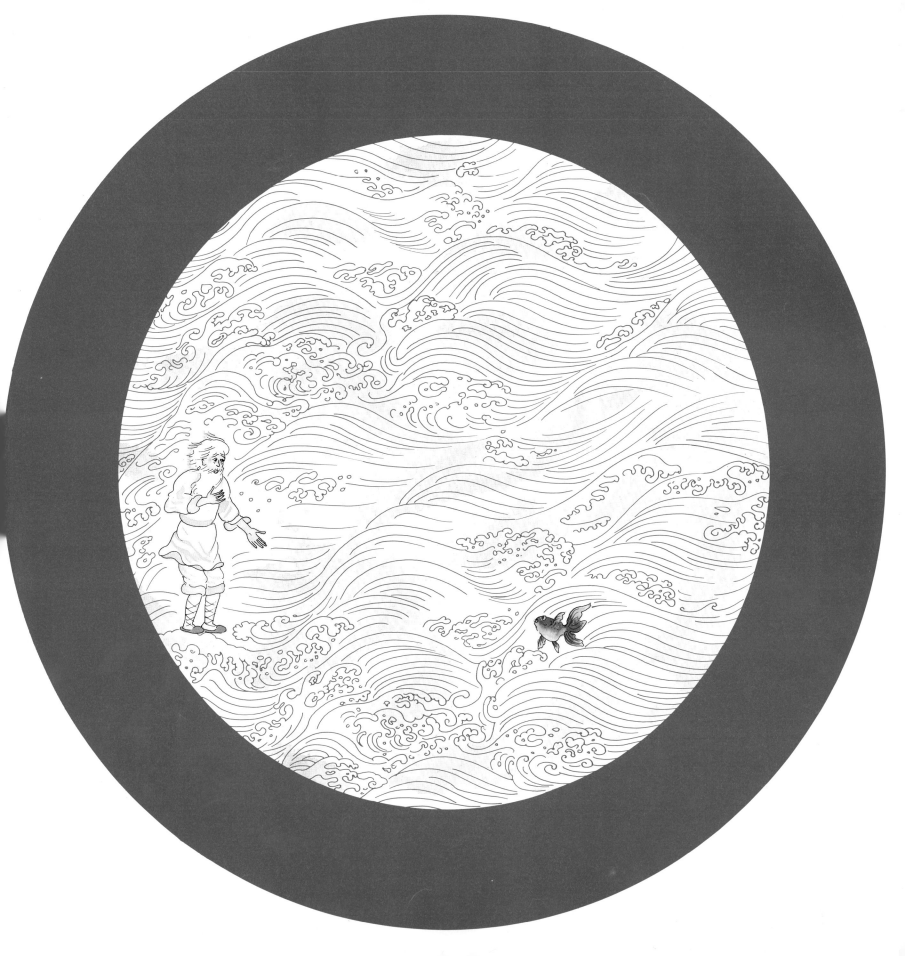

To his wife the old fisherman hastened.
And what did he see? A tall mansion,
And in it, his wife as a Lady,
With shoes of the softest red leather.
Her headdress in gold was embroidered;
Her necklace had diamonds and rubies,
And her fingers were ringed with fine jewels.
The old man approached his wife saying:
"O greetings, Your Ladyship! Greetings!
I hope that your soul's now contented."
She angrily bade him be silent
And sent him to serve in the stables.

A week slowly passed, then another.
The woman grew prouder than ever.
One morning she sent for her husband:
"Go bow to the Gold Fish and tell it
I'm tired of being a Lady—
I shall be made queen—a Czarina!"
Her husband implored her in terror:
"Old woman, you've surely gone crazy!
You can't even talk like a Lady.
You'll be mocked all over the kingdom!"
The woman grew madder than ever,
Slapped his face, and shouted in fury:
"How dare a peasant argue with me,
A Lady so fine—a Fine Lady?
Return to the Gold Fish, I warn you,
Or be dragged to the seashore by force!"

The old man went down to the seashore.

The ocean was swollen and sullen.

He called to the magical Gold Fish.

The Gold Fish swam right up and asked him:

"What is it, old man, you are wanting?

Then bowing, the old man did answer:

"Forgive me, Your Majesty Gold Fish!

Again my old woman's gone crazy.

She's tired of being a Lady,

She wants to be made a Czarina!"

The Gold Fish did not smile, but answered:

"Very well, she'll be a Czarina.

Don't worry. Go home. God be with you!"

To his wife the old fisherman hastened.
And what did he see? A grand palace.
And on the great throne—his old wife!
She drank from a goblet of gold,
And ate gingerbread from silver dishes.
Around her grim guards stood in silence.
The old man bowed down and said humbly:
"Greetings, O Mighty Czarina!
I hope now your soul is contented."
But she gave not a glance at her husband—
She ordered him thrust from her presence.
A week slowly passed, then another.
Then she sent for her husband one morning.
"Go back to the Gold Fish and tell it
I'm tired of being a Czarina—
Of the seas I'll be mistress instead!
And my servant—the magical Gold Fish!"

The old man dared not contradict her
Or open his lips in an answer.
He sadly set out for the seashore.
A tempest raged over the ocean;
The waters were roiling and angry;
And billows were foaming with fury!
He called to the magical Gold Fish.
The Gold Fish swam right up and asked him:
"What is it you want now, old man?"
Then bowing, the old man did answer:
"Forgive me, Your Majesty Gold Fish!
My cursed old woman's still angry.
She's tried of being a Czarina,
She wants of the seas to be mistress
And her servant: Your Majesty Gold Fish!"

Not a word spoke the Gold Fish in answer,
But swishing his tail, and in silence,
Disappeared to the depths of the ocean.
The old man did wait for an answer,
And at last turned his steps to the palace.
But behold! There again stood his hovel
—On the doorstep sat his old wife,
With the same broken washtub before her!

Author's Note

This version of Aleksandr Pushkin's
"The Tale of the Fisherman and the Little
Fish" is adapted from Louis Zelikoff's
masterful translation. I consulted many
English-language versions of this story, but
Zelikoff's I found to be the most accessible
for children.